MW00892034

Codex Regius
Dynasties of Middle-earth
Kings, lords and other noblemen from the First to the Third Age

Codex Regius

Dynasties
of Middle-earth

**Kings, lords and other noblemen
from the First to the Third Age**

Non-fiction

1ᵗ edition

Wiesbaden/Ljubljana 2014

Published by: © 2015 Codex Regius

Printed by CreateSpace

Also available for Kindle and other devices

All rights reserved.

Authors: Codex Regius

Contact: codex.regius@romanike.de

Cover and layout: Codex Regius

All images from public domain

Maps and diagrams designed by Codex Regius

This book, including its parts, is protected by copyright and may not be reproduced, resold or forwarded without approval of the author.

Cover image: The tree of generations

Introduction

This book is a revision and expansion of a PDF file that I kept for a couple of years on **Lalaith's Middle-earth Science Pages** (http://homepage.o2mail. de/Lalaith/M-earth.html). It comprises the genealogical trees of the noble Mannish houses from the First to the Fourth Age of J.R.R. Tolkien's Middle-earth that are not found in the Appendices of 'The Lord of the Rings' or 'The Silmarillion' but spread over various sources which sometimes conflict with each other.

Represented are: the Houses of the Edain, the Line of Elros (including the lords of Hyarastorni and Andunië), the Heirs of Elendil with the lords of Umbar, the noble Houses of Emyn Arnen and Dol Amroth, the Lords of the Éothéod, the Kings of Rohan, the Lords of Aldburg and the Lords and Kings of Dale. And then there is that odd fellow who does not fit into any of these tables: King Bladorthin, whose likely fate is discussed in another volume derived from Lalaith's Middle-earth Science Pages: 'Middle-earth seen by the barbarians, Vol. 1'.

The tables are compiled from five main sources that have been weighted by plausibility: Tables 1-3 draw heavily on 'The Silmarillion' (**S**), the others on 'The Lord of the Rings' (**LR**). Many dates, additional family members etc. were found in 'The War of the Jewels' (**WJ**), 'Unfinished Tales' (**UT**) and 'The Peoples of Middle-earth' (**PM**).

Each table is accompanied by short references to the main historical events that concerned the dynastic members. Commentaries discuss the lifespans and the succession of generations among the royal bloodlines or remark on inconsistencies in the available source texts.

For the sake of concise presentation, the nomenclature of the **LR** prologue was adopted, giving the age (First, Second, Third, Fourth) in Roman numerals and the year in Arabic numerals. Hence, *III 3019* corresponds to the year 3019 TA (Third Age).

In the tradition of Rohan, the royal dynasties were treated as separate 'lines' whenever direct male descent was disrupted. This custom had quite a physical meaning to the Rohirrim: each time a new line started, a new row of mounds was begun on the royal cemetery. For the matter of this presentation, it has been found convenient to apply similar distinctions to other recorded dynasties, though such have not been officially stated.

Signs used in the tables:

* date of birth
† date of death by natural cause
‡ date of death by unnatural cause
v last reported alive
● date of ascension
○ date of leaving or losing the throne

Ruling kings or lords are set in vertically opening scrolls, other members of the noble houses in horizontal scrolls. Members who entered a house by marriage are shown in boxes with rounded corners.

List of Abbreviations

AA 'The Annals of Aman', in: The War of the Jewels, 1994.

AD 'Aelfwine and Dírhaval' in: The War of the Jewels, 1994.

AE 'Aldarion and Erendis' in: Unfinished Tales, 1980.

AF 'Atrabeth Finrod ah Andreth', in: Morgoth's Ring, 1993.

AG 'Of Tuor and his Arrival in Gondolin' in: Unfinished Tales, 1980.

AI J.R.R. Tolkien - Artist and Illustrator, by W. Hammond and Chr. Scull, 1995.

AK 'The Akallabêth' in: The Silmarillion, 1977.

AL 'The Appendix on Languages', in: The Peoples of Middle earth, 1996.

ATB The Adventures of Tom Bombadil, 1961

CE 'Cirion and Éorl' in: Unfinished Tales, 1980.

CG The Complete Guide to Middle-earth, by R. Foster, 1978.

Co The Tolkien Companion, by J. E. A. Tyler, 1976.

DA 'The Drowning of Anadune', in: Sauron Defeated, 1991.

DM 'Of Dwarves and Men', in: The Peoples of Middle earth, 1996.

DN 'A Description of Númenor' in: Unfinished Tales, 1980.

EL 'Tar-Elmar' in: The Peoples of Middle earth, 1996.

FI 'The Battles at the Fords of Isen' in: Unfinished Tales, 1980.

FR The Fellowship of the Ring, 1965.

GA 'The Grey Annals' in: The War of the Jewels, 1994.

GC 'The History of Galadriel and Celeborn' in: Unfinished Tales, 1980.

GF 'The Disaster of the Gladden Fields' in: Unfinished Tales, 1980.

GN 'Guide to the Names in the Lord of the Rings', in: A Tolkien Compass, by J. Lobdell, 1974

H The Hobbit or There and Back Again, 1937 (chapters in roman numerals)

HA 'The History of the Akallabêth', in: The Peoples of Middle earth, 1996.

HE 'The Heirs of Elendil', in: The Peoples of Middle earth, 1996

HH 'Narn i Hín Húrin' in: Unfinished Tales, 1980.

HoMe The History of Middle-earth. Vol. I to XII.

HR 'The Hunt for the Ring' in: Unfinished Tales, 1980.

KR 'Annals of the Kings and Rulers', Appendix A in: The Return of the King, 1965.

L# Letter No. #, in: The Letters of J.R.R. Tolkien, 1981.

LE 'The Line of Elros' in: Unfinished Tales, 1980.

LP 'The Languages and Peoples of the Third Age', Appendix F in: The Return of the King, 1965.

LQ 'The Later Quenta Silmarillion' in: The War of the Jewels, 1994.

LR The Lord of the Rings, 1965 ff.

LW 'Last Writings: The Five Wizards', in: The Peoples of Middle earth, 1996.

MR Morgoth's Ring, The History of Middle-earth, Vol. X, 1993.

MT 'Myths Transformed', in: Morgoth's Ring, 1993.

NC 'The Notion Club Papers', in: Sauron Defeated, 1991.

NE 'Of the Naugrim and the Edain', in: The War of the Jewels, 1994

PM The Peoples of Middle-earth, The History of Middle-earth, Vol. XII, 1996.

PR 'The Problem of Ros', in: The Peoples of Middle earth, 1996.

QE 'The Quest for Erebor' in: Unfinished Tales, 1980.

QS 'The Later Quenta Silmarillion', in: The War of the Jewels, 1994

Q&A 'Quendi and Eldar', in: The War of the Jewels, 1994

RA Lowdham`s Report on Adunaic, in: Sauron Defeated, 1991.

RK The Return of the King, 1965.

RP 'Of the Rings of Power and the Third Age' in: The Silmarillion, 1977.

RS The Return of the Shadow, The History of Middle-earth, Vol. VI, 1988

S The Silmarillion, 1977.

TA 'The Ainulindalë', in: The Silmarillion, 1977.

TC 'The Calendars ', Appendix D in: The Return of the King, 1965.

TD 'The Drúedain' in: Unfinished Tales, 1980.

TE 'The Etymologies', in: The Lost Road and other Writings, 1987.

TG 'Of Tuor and his Arrival in Gondolin', in: Unfinished Tales, 1980.

TI 'The Istari', in: Unfinished Tales, 1980.

TM The Atlas of Middle-earth, by K.W. Fonstad, 1981/1991.

TR The Treason of Isengard, The History of Middle-earth, Vol. VII, 1989

TT The Two Towers, 1965.

TY 'The Tale of Years', Appendix B in: The Return of the King, 1965.

UT Unfinished Tales, 1980.

WH 'The Wanderings of Húrin' in: The War of the Jewels, 1994.

WJ The War of the Jewels, The History of Middle-earth, Vol. XI, 1994.

WP 'Word, Phrases and Passages in various tongues in The Lord of the Rings', in: Gilson, Ch.: Parma Eldalamberon 17, 2007

WS 'Writing and Spelling', Appendix E in: The Return of the King, 1965.

YF 'The Tale of Years [of the First Age]', in: The War of the Jewels, 1994

YS 'The Tale of Years of the Second Age', in: The Peoples of Middle earth, 1996

YT 'The Tale of Years of the Third Age', in: The Peoples of Middle earth, 1996

FA First Age

SA Second Age

TA Third Age

Table 1: The House of Bëor (bar Bëora)

The Legends of the Elder Days have never been published in a finished narrative. The following tables 1 to 3 are therefore only attempts to record the state in which the genealogies of the three Houses of the Edain were 'frozen' rather than completed. The latest revision of the genealogical table presented in **WJ** has been adopted and its data supplemented by those of the published **S**. Note that many names are only found in this table and do not occur in any story.

Even at this early stage in history, the average life expectancy of Edain from the First House was, surprisingly, 90 years while a turn of generations was rather conventional: about 25 years. This would mean that about 10 generations had passed from the Awakening of Man to the birth of Bëor the Old. He should still have remembered people who had been born about 170 of the First Age. It is somewhat difficult to understand, therefore, why all precise knowledge of the first Fall of Mankind had been lost rather than devoted to tradition.

The chronological data of main events given in **WJ** have been verified against those of **S** as printed, with **S** receiving preference where applicable. These data seem to confirm a couple of calculations that had been presented in **CG**, deriving from data in the published **S** only, but there are increasing deviations for the late First Age after 460 FA.

The year when Bëor the Old died was first guessed at in **CG** but later confirmed by **QS**. Based on this reference year, it is possible to calculate back on the years in which the Haladin and the People of Marach entered Beleriand.

Since there was much mingling with the Second House of the Edain, all the male lines of the House of Bëor that had dwelt in Beleriand were extinct by the end of the First Age, unless Belegor had any unrecorded descendants that may have continued the line. A Bëorian minority, however, was still found in the West of the island of Númenor, according to some sources, though their number was small and they had merged with the majority by the end of the Age.

All dates given are FA.

Problems and discrepancies

Andreth: Her actual year of death is not recorded. Finrod Felagund prophecies in **AF** that she would outlive the Noldorian king Aegnor, who fell in the Dagor Bragollach, 455 FA. Andreth was 94 years old at that time and may not have lived much longer than that.

Bereg: He left Beleriand with 1000 of his people, and nothing more of his fate is known. Quite probably, he and his followers contributed to the native peoples who were discovered by the Númenóreans in Eriador, later in the Second Age (their history is told in 'Middle-earth seen by the barbarians, Vol. 1').

Beren (elder) : The son of Belemir was named fifth child in an older genealogy of the House of Bëor (**LQ**). The reference was not deliberately rejected, however, and therefore it has been assumed here as still applying.

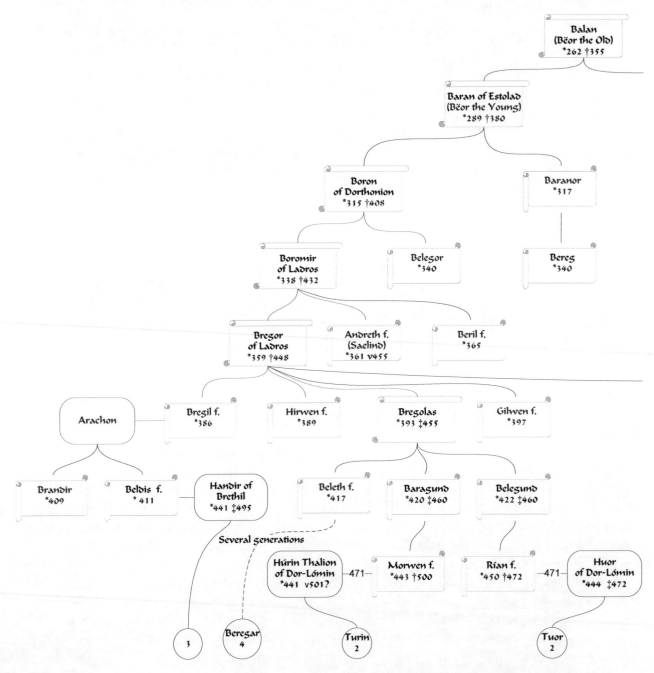

Balan
(Bëor the Old)
*262 †355

Baran of Estolad
(Bëor the Young)
*289 †380

Boron
of Dorthonion
*315 †408

Baranor
*317

Boromir
of Ladros
*338 †432

Belegor
*340

Bereg
*340

Bregor
of Ladros
*359 †448

Andreth f.
(Saelind)
*361 v455

Beril f.
*365

Arachon

Bregil f.
*386

Hirwen f.
*389

Bregolas
*393 ‡455

Gilwen f.
*397

Brandir
*409

Beldis f.
*411

Handir of
Brethil
*441 ‡495

Beleth f.
*417

Baragund
*420 ‡460

Belegund
*422 ‡460

Several generations

Húrin Thalion
of Dor-Lómin
*441 v501?

—471—

Morwen f.
*443 †500

Rían f.
*450 †472

—471—

Huor
of Dor-Lómin
*444 ‡472

3

Beregar
4

Turin
2

Tuor
2

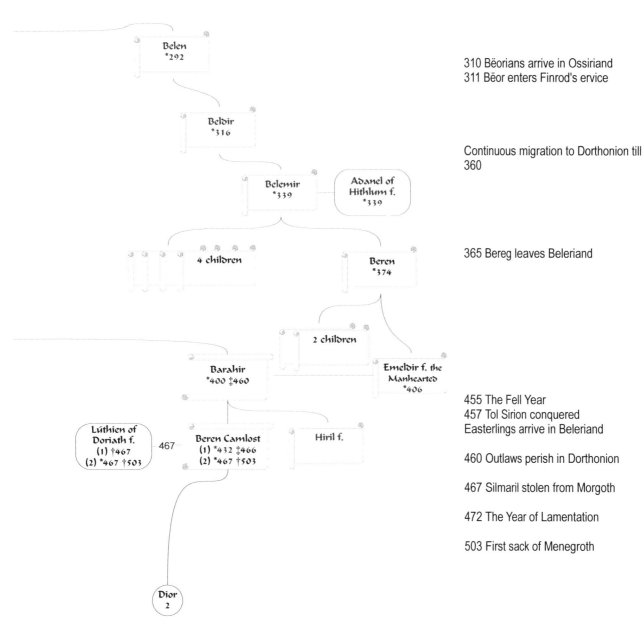

Belen
*292

Beldir
*316

Belemir
*339

Adanel of
Hithlum f.
*339

4 children

Beren
*374

2 children

Barahir
*400 ‡460

Emeldir f. the
Manhearteð
*406

Lúthien of
Doriath f.
(1) †467
(2) *467 †503

467

Beren Camlost
(1) *432 ‡466
(2) *467 †503

Hiril f.

Dior
2

310 Bëorians arrive in Ossiriand
311 Bëor enters Finrod's ervice

Continuous migration to Dorthonion till
360

365 Bereg leaves Beleriand

455 The Fell Year
457 Tol Sirion conquered
Easterlings arrive in Beleriand

460 Outlaws perish in Dorthonion

467 Silmaril stolen from Morgoth

472 The Year of Lamentation

503 First sack of Menegroth

Table 2a: The People of Marach (nothlir Maracha), afterwards called the House of Hador

This is the most complex genealogical table of the First Age. It is also the one that is most extensively discussed in **S** and **UT**, so that many data could be collected from there which only needed verification and supplements from **WJ**.

A peculiar oddity is the intrusion of a non-Elvish-sounding name, Zimrahin, said to derive from the original language that the People of Marach spoke. Its sound pattern is clearly reminiscent of Adûnaic, the language of Númenor, where compound elements like *Zimra-* were abundant (see the separate book 'Words of Westernesse' for details). For that reason, probably, there is the explicit statement found that the Hadorians retained their native language, unlike the Bëorians who gave up their closely related tongue and adopted Sindarin as their everyday speech.

Another curious phenomenon among the People of Marach is the militaristic baptising of their sons: Magor 'the Sword' - Hathol 'the Axe' - Hador 'the Warrior', as the names are translated in **WJ**. They do not actually sound as if their fathers had been very content with the Long Peace of Beleriand.

A late revision indicated in **WJ** exchanged Magor and his grandson Hathor in the table. Since this suggestion had no consequences for other texts and would introduce a huge discrepancy with the published **S**, this modification was not adopted here.

Unless otherwise stated, all dates given are FA.

Problems and discrepancies

Húrin: **S** states that he died at the age of 65 years. In **GA** this was correctly amended to 66, in accordance with the genealogies in **WJ**.

Aerin: She does not appear in any genealogical table. The reason may be that she was changed very late from a 'kinswoman of Morwen' (**GA**), i.e. of the House of Bëor, to a relative 'of Húrin' (**S**). In 495 FA, she was a white-haired Lady. Túrin called her his aunt in **HH**. It is therefore reasonable to assume that 'kinswoman' meant she was of the same generation as Húrin and that her father Indor, called in the **UT Index** only 'man of Dor-Lómin', was very likely a cousin of Galdor and Gundor (as his name suggests). Aerin burnt Brodda's hall in 495 FA. It is not known whether she died as well on that occasion.

Nienor: Received a child from her brother and husband Túrin but committed suicide before birth, therefore this child is not listed here.

Dírhavel: Said in **AD** to be a descendant of the House of Hador. In this case, only Gundor could be his ancestor because all the descendants of Galdor are accounted for. Perhaps this statement should rather read 'House of Marach'?

Table 2b: The Half-Elves

The ancestry of the Half-Elves was absolutely unique in the world: It included all three Houses of the Edain, the Noldor of Gondolin, the Sindar of Doriath and, last but not least, a corporeal Ainu. This profound mixture of mortal Men, immortal Elves and even a semi-divine being (Melian of Doriath), it is said, led to the only reasonably founded claim of nobility among Mannish rulers. Bloodline became a concern that was observed for ages after. People later said of noble men as 'the blood of Númenor was running true in them', though that was no warrant of adequate moral behaviour, as cases like Ar-Pharazôn or Castamir of Umbar have shown.

When Eärendil married Elwing, the sole survivor of Beren's descendants, the Half-Elves of the First Age were united in a single line, sorting out a problem of increasing concern to the Valar: Should they be reckoned as immortal Elves or as mortal Men? (The impending population with further Half-Elves by Túrin and his Noldorin girlfriend Finduilas of Nargothrond had been prevented in time. By Glaurung the Dragon.)

In the end, a choice was given to the twin sons Elros and Elrond, and they took fates that were much different from each other until their separate lines were united again by Arwen marrying her own remote nephew by many generations - an incest separated by several milleniums!

Still, a satisfying solution to the postumous fate of Half-Elves did not seem to have been achieved. The King's Men of Númenor had a point when they asked whether Elros had made the right decision and why it could not be reverted. And why did Elrond's children have a choice but not Elros'?

Perhaps Ar-Pharazôn (table 7) had taught a lesson to the Valar after all: Since all children of Elrond were born after his rebellion, it may seem that because of him the initial decision to grant the Choice only to the sons of Eärendil and Elwing was revised. Still, it would seem odd that the three children had in a way the best of both worlds, since they were under no pressure to make their decision soon and left the issue pending for several milleniums.

And as sound as this guess may seem, it leaves the matter of the Princes of Dol Amroth (table 15) unanswered. Should not the scion of Imrazôr the Númenorean (a man) and Mithrellas (an Elf) have been a Half-Elf as well and earned a choice by birthright?

Ultimately, it was Eru who had to decide whether a Choice was granted, the Valar could only propose. And the pattern is familiar: Whenever Eru intervenes, justice is elsewhere.

Unless otherwise stated, all dates given are FA.

Problems and discrepancies

Díor: The date of the second Sack of Menegroth and the perishing of Díor's family is once given as 506 in **WJ,** but another time it is stated as 511. **S** reckons the Fall of Gondolin in 510 FA, and it is explicitly said that this catastrophe happened *after* the ruin of Doriath. For that reason, 506 is the date accepted in this table.

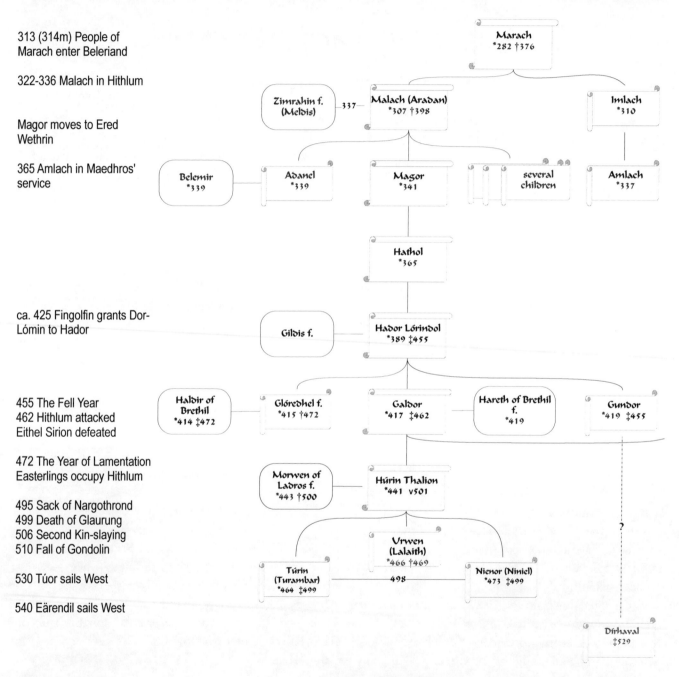

313 (314m) People of Marach enter Beleriand

322-336 Malach in Hithlum

Magor moves to Ered Wethrin

365 Amlach in Maedhros' service

ca. 425 Fingolfin grants Dor-Lómin to Hador

455 The Fell Year
462 Hithlum attacked Eithel Sirion defeated

472 The Year of Lamentation Easterlings occupy Hithlum

495 Sack of Nargothrond
499 Death of Glaurung
506 Second Kin-slaying
510 Fall of Gondolin

530 Túor sails West

540 Eärendil sails West

Marach
*282 †376

Zimrahin f. (Meldis) —337— Malach (Aradan) *307 †398

Imlach *310

Belemir *339 — Adanel *339

Magor *341

several children

Amlach *337

Hathol *365

Gildis f. — Hador Lórindol *389 ‡455

Haldir of Brethil *414 ‡472 — Glóredhel f. *415 †472

Galdor *417 ‡462 — Hareth of Brethil f. *419

Gundor *419 ‡455

Morwen of Ladros f. *443 †500 — Húrin Thalion *441 v501

?

Túrin (Turambar) *464 ‡499 —498—

Urwen (Lalaith) *466 †469

Nienor (Niniel) *473 ‡499

Dírhaval ‡529

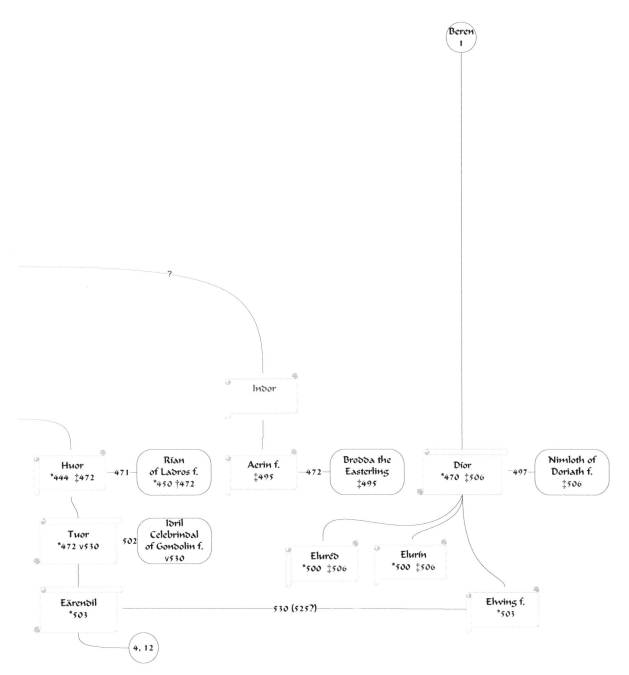

Beren
1

?

Indor

Huor
*444 ‡472

—471—

Rían
of Ladros f.
*450 †472

Aerin f.
‡495

—472—

Brodda the
Easterling
‡495

Díor
*470 ‡506

—497—

Nimloth of
Doriath f.
‡506

Tuor
*472 v530

Idril
Celebrindal
of Gondolin f.
v530

502

Eluréd
*500 ‡506

Elurín
*500 ‡506

Eärendil
*503

———530 (525?)———

Elwing f.
*503

4, 12

Table 3: The People of Haleth (nothlir Haletha) or Haladin

These people were last of the Edain to come to Beleriand. They evidently suffered from low fertility, so that their genealogical tree is rather thin in comparison, in spite of their average lifespan being as long as that of the much more populous Hadorians.

Beside the House of Hador, this is the second example of a tribe that has changed its eponymic name to honour a popular hero - or in that case, a heroine. According to **WJ**, it has not been finally established whether their alternate name, *Haladin*, referred to the whole people or just to a special caste among them. One suggestion was that *Haladin* was actually a word that meant 'warden'.

The fact that the language of the People of Haleth was entirely unrelated to that of the other Edain suggests to ask the question how such a profound gap may have developed within the less than three centuries that had passed since the Awakening of Man. While the Elves had undergone a long process of linguistic development and education by the more exploratively minded Valar (and they were immortal, at any rate), Men awoke without any such guidance, so they must have been equipped with languages by Eru already.

But why several languages? There is no analogon to the Tower-of-Babel incident in ancient Middle-earth, and the mutual incomprehensibility of the Edain was acting to the detriment of the Haladin and their relatives in Eriador and Gondor who were later often lumped together with the Men of Darkness and treated like inferior peoples or even thralls of Evil, though they were in fact kinsmen of the Edain (see 'Middle-earth seen by the barbarians, Vol. 1'). Once again: Whenever Eru intervenes, justice is obviously elsewhere.

The main source of information on the People of Haleth is **S,** with additional data supplied by **QS** and **WH**.

The notion that the ruling House of Haleth went extinct with Manthor (500 FA) is only found in **WH**. Afterwards, the Haladin of Brethil were ruled by 'lesser men' (**WH**) who probably stayed in charge until the War of Wrath. Nothing about them has ever been told.

312 or 313 Haladin enter Ossiriand

375 Orc-raid in Thargelion

Haleth leads Haladin to Brethil

455 The Fell Year
Brethil defended

472 The Year of Lamentation

495 Battle of Tumhalad

500 End of the House of Haleth
"Lesser men" begin to rule Brethil

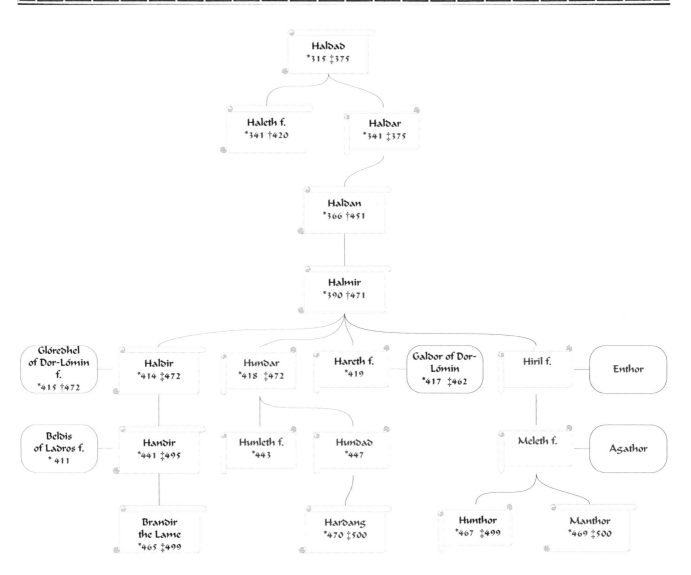

Table 4: The first Line of Elros

32 Edain reach Númenor

This table covers the early Mannish descendants of Eärendil. For his Elvish descendants, see table 12.

The first Line of Elros has been recorded to some extent in **AE**. After that, our main genealogical source is **KR** which gives the names of kings but not the dates of their lives. These have mostly been taken from **LE**, a few of them can be verified by comparison with **TY**. Alas, these documents rarely list wives, siblings or other relatives. It is only said that after Tar-Anárion, all heirs to the throne married other descendants of the Line of Elros in an attempt to maintain genetic purity.

Unless otherwise stated, all dates given are SA.

Problems and discrepancies

Elros: Both **KR** and **LE** state that Elros was born 58 years before the End of the First Age. Alas, this date has never been finally established. His date of birth is given as 532 in **WJ**. In agreement with these statements, the End of the First Age was accepted as 590 FA.

Silmariën: Older editions of **TY** give her birth-date as 548 but **LE** as 521. Since she is attested as the eldest child of Tar-Elendil, accepting the peculiar **TY** value would require waiving the recorded birth dates of her younger siblings as well. In editions following 2004, **TY** was amended to 521.

Name	born	died	lived	generation
Vardamir	61	471	410	119
Tar-Amandil	192	603	411	131
Tar-Elendil	350	751	401	158
Tar-Meneldur	543	942	399	193
Tar-Aldarion	700	1098	398	157
Tar-Ancalime	873	1285	412	173
Tar-Anárion	1003	1404	401	130
Tar-Súrion	1174	1574	400	171
Tar-Telperien	1320	1731	411	146
Tar-Minastir	1474	1873	399	154

600 Vëantur returns to Middle-earth

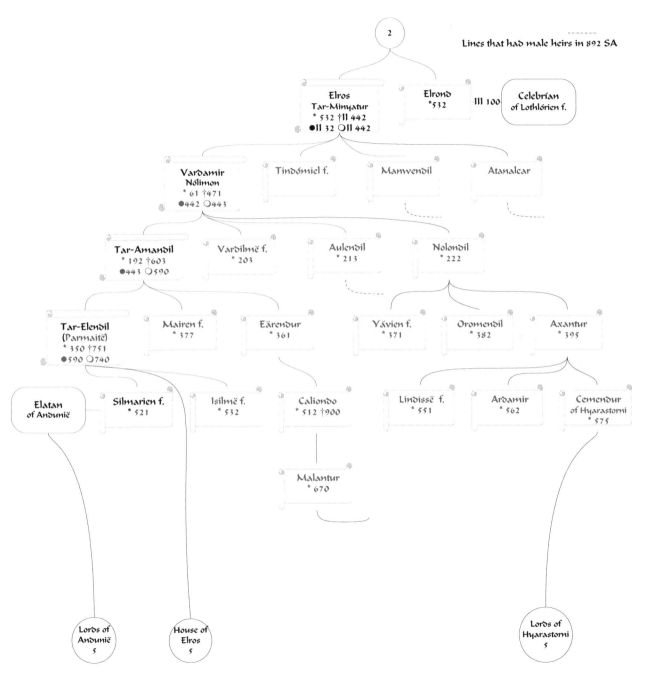

Lines that had male heirs in 892 SA

2

Elros
Tar-Minyatur
* 532 †II 442
●II 32 ○II 442

Elrond
*532

III 100

Celebrían
of Lothlórien f.

Vardamir
Nólimon
* 61 †471
●442 ○443

Tindómiel f.

Manwendil

Atanalcar

Tar-Amandil
* 192 †603
●443 ○590

Vardilmë f.
* 203

Aulendil
* 213

Nolondil
* 222

Tar-Elendil
(Parmaitë)
* 350 †751
●590 ○740

Mairen f.
* 377

Eärendur
* 361

Yávien f.
* 371

Oromendil
* 382

Axantur
* 395

Elatan
of Andunië

Silmarien f.
* 521

Isilmë f.
* 532

Caliondo
* 512 †900

Lindissë f.
* 551

Ardamir
* 562

Cemendur
of Hyarastorni
* 575

Malantur
* 670

Lords of
Andunië
5

House of
Elros
5

Lords of
Hyarastorni
5

17

Table 5a: The first line of Elros

This table continues the genealogical tree of table 4 to the end of the first line with Tar-Telperiën who died childless. The main source is **LE,** with remote relatives added from **AE**.

The spreadsheet of the Line of Elros shows that a generation counted initially about 140 years, rising to 170 in the 2nd millenium and dropping to 80 when the Shadow falls on Númenor.

After the first Lord of Andunië, a port in the west of Númenor, the names and any birth or death dates of his line are lost in time till the 15th lord who lived in the late 3rd millenium. Only the number of ruling lords has survived.

It was tentatively assumed that 140 years was also the average length of a generation in the house of the Lords of Andunië. Entering the resulting hypothetical values gives an almost perfect set of conjectural birth years down to the last lord, Elendil. These years are given in this and the following tables. We will see that they help resolve a few problems in the later genealogy of the Line of Elros.

Unless otherwise stated, all dates given are SA.

Problems and discrepancies

Tar-Telperiën: A problem with the lifespans seems to have arisen here. As pointed out in **LE**, her death-date as given does not agree with the attested date of her nephew Tar-Minastir's interference into the War of the Elves and Sauron (1700 SA). The date of Tar-Minastir's ascension is consistent with Tar-Telperiën's surrender of the sceptre, however. We may perhaps assume that according to the present concept, Tar-Minastir has sent the navy of Númenor to help the Elves in his function as hereditary prince and fleet commander, not yet in the position of a king, though he is called 'Tar-Minastir the King' when the event is described in **GC**. His aunt may have accepted him as vicegerent before she fully surrendered the sceptre to him. There is nothing in any extant text that would support such a suggestion, however.

Hallacar of Hyarastorni: In the official records, only Hallacar is named 'of Hyarastorni'. But it is probable that the line was already existing before him, coming down from the eldest male descendants.

750 Guild of Venturers founded

892 Change of succession law
Foundation of Vinyalondë

1000 Sauron enters Mordor

1200 Many Númenorean havens founded in Middle-earth

1600 Barad-dûr completed
1693-1700 War of the Elves and Sauron

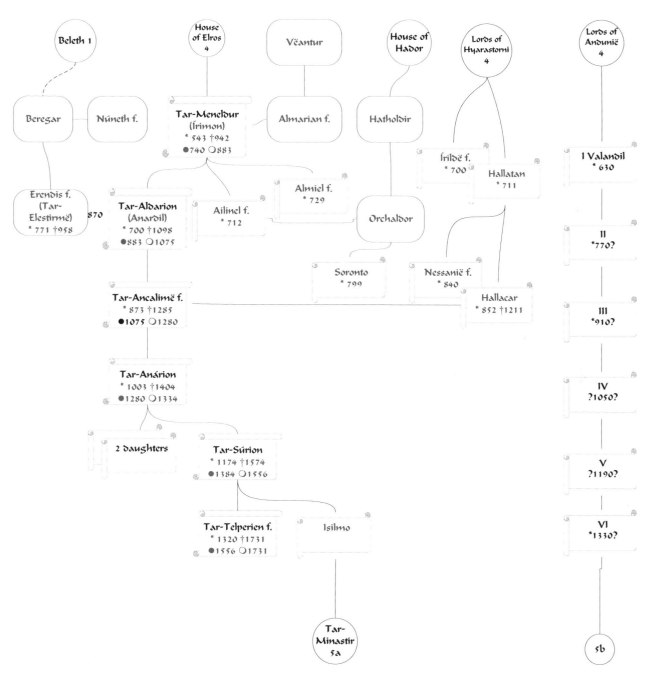

Beleth 1

Beregar

Núneth f.

House of Elros 4

Tar-Meneldur
(Írimon)
* 543 †942
●740 ○883

Vëantur

Almarian f.

House of Hador

Hatholdir

Lords of Hyarastorni 4

Írildë f.
* 700

Hallatan
* 711

Lords of Andunië 4

I Valandil
* 630

Erendis f.
(Tar-Elestirmë)
* 771 †958

870

Tar-Aldarion
(Anardil)
* 700 †1098
●883 ○1075

Ailinel f.
* 712

Almiel f.
* 729

Orchaldor

II
*770?

Soronto
* 799

Nessanië f.
* 840

Tar-Ancalimë f.
* 873 †1285
●1075 ○1280

Hallacar
* 852 †1211

III
*910?

Tar-Anárion
* 1003 †1404
●1280 ○1334

IV
?1050?

2 daughters

Tar-Súrion
* 1174 †1574
●1384 ○1556

V
?1190?

Tar-Telperien f.
* 1320 †1731
●1556 ○1731

Isilmo

VI
*1330?

Tar-Minastir
5a

5b

Table 6: The second line (descendants of Isilmo) in the Age of Glory

The lines of the House of Elros and of the next Lords of Andunië continue from the previous table.

The spreadsheet shows a distinct difference between the First and the Second Line: While the kings of the First Line received their heirs at the age of 130 or 140, those of the Second Line take much longer: 150 to 160 years. Tar-Atanamir holds the record: he could not only have been called the Great but also the Old, for he lived longer than any king since Elros or after, and nobody received a heir later than he: He was 186 when Tar-Ancalimon was finally born!

With Tar-Telemmaitë, the generations begin to shorten, as does the lifespan of the Line of Elros.

Problems and discrepancies

Tar-Atanamir: Older editions of **TY** erroneously give 2251 as the date of his ascension. This was corrected in editions from 2004.

Tar-Anducal: He acted as regent and assumed the throne after his wife's death. His inclusion as official king of Númenor, however, is contested (**LE**).

1800 Dominions founded. Shadow falls on Númenor

Population divides between King's Men and Elf-friends

2280 Umbar fortified.
2350 Faithful found Pelargir.

Name	born	died	lived	generation
Tar-Ciryatan	1634	2035	401	160
Tar-Atanamir	1800	2251	451	166
Tar-Ancalimon	1986	2386	400	186
Tar-Telemmaitë	2136	2526	390	150
Tar-Vanimeldë	2277	2637	360	141
Tar-Alcarin	2406	2737	331	129
Tar-Calmacil	2516	2825	309	110

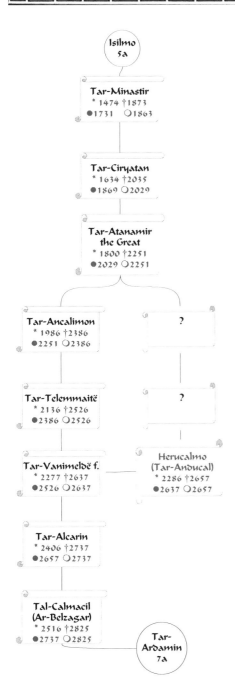

Isilmo
5a

Tar-Minastir
* 1474 †1873
●1731 ○1863

Tar-Ciryatan
* 1634 †2035
●1869 ○2029

**Tar-Atanamir
the Great**
* 1800 †2251
●2029 ○2251

Tar-Ancalimon
* 1986 †2386
●2251 ○2386

?

Tar-Telemmaitë
* 2136 †2526
●2386 ○2526

?

Tar-Vanimeldë f.
* 2277 †2637
●2526 ○2637

**Herucalmo
(Tar-Anducal)**
* 2286 †2657
●2637 ○2657

Tar-Alcarin
* 2406 †2737
●2657 ○2737

**Tal-Calmacil
(Ar-Belzagar)**
* 2516 †2825
●2737 ○2825

Tar-
Ardamin
7a

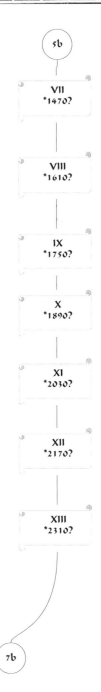

5b

VII
*1470?

VIII
*1610?

IX
*1750?

X
*1890?

XI
*2030?

XII
*2170?

XIII
*2310?

7b

Table 7: The second line (descendants of Isilmo) under the Shadow

In the age under the Shadow, the generations shorten below 100 years, approaching an average of 80 years for the last kings. Lifespans shorten as well, approaching little more than 200 years, which is the life expectation of a commoner in the early ages of Númenor ('thrice the span of mortal Men in Middle-earth').

The main sources are again **KR** and **LE**; additions to the final generations have been taken from **HA**.

Problems and discrepancies

Tar-Ardamin was missing from all editions of **KR** published before 2004. CT wondered in a comment to **LE** whether this king really belonged into the list because Ar-Adûnakhôr was attested as the first king who wrote his throne name in the Adûnaic language. In fact, it is evident that Tar-Ardamin's name must have been dropped from the namelist in **KR** by accident: otherwise **KR** and **LE** could not agree that Ar-Adûnakhôr was the twentieth King of Númenor.

The statement in **KR** had to be corrected: It was not after Tar-Calmacil but after Tar-Ardamin that the Kings chose to assume names in Adûnaic on ascension. This was corrected in editions from 2004.

Gimilkhâd is attested by **A** as having lived 98 years. He did not live to his 99th birthday that would have been due in 3243.

Ar-Gimilzôr's date of death is given by **TY** as 3175 but by **LE** as 3177. CT thinks that 3175 is correct.

Inzilbêth: Genealogical tables that have not been published so far make her the daughter of Tar-Ardamin's brother Gimilzagar. This is not as impossible as suggested in **LE**. It could simply mean that Gimilzagar was of high age when Inzilbêth was born and that she was in turn much older than Ar-Gimilzôr, though not irrationally old. The influence of her memories may have been the secret behind Tar-Palantir's odd repentance.

3175 Repentance of Tar-Palantir. Civil war.

3261 Ar-Pharazôn at Umbar
3262 Sauron taken prisoner
3319 Downfall of Númenor
3320 Realms in Exile founded

3430-3441 War of the Last Alliance

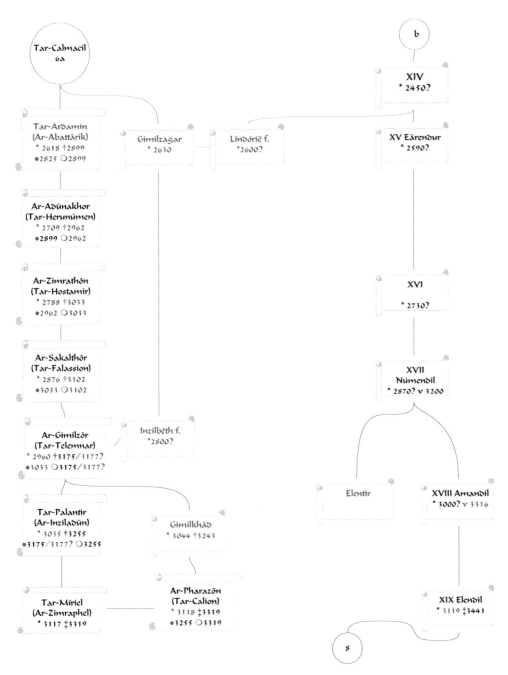

Tar-Calmacil
6a

Tar-Ardamin
(Ar-Abattârik)
* 2618 †2899
●2825 ○2899

Gimilzagar
* 2630

Lindórië f.
*2600?

b

XIV
* 2450?

XV Eärendur
* 2590?

Ar-Adûnakhor
(Tar-Herunúmen)
* 2709 †2962
●2899 ○2962

Ar-Zimrathôn
(Tar-Hostamir)
* 2788 †3033
●2962 ○3033

XVI
* 2730?

Ar-Sakalthôr
(Tar-Falassion)
* 2876 †3102
●3033 ○3102

XVII
Númendil
* 2870? v 3200

Ar-Gimilzôr
(Tar-Telemnar)
* 2960 †3175/3177?
●3033 ○3175/3177?

Inzilbêth f.
*2800?

Tar-Palantir
(Ar-Inziladûn)
* 3035 †3255
●3175/3177? ○3255

Gimilkhâd
* 3044 †3243

Elentir

XVIII Amandil
* 3000? v 3316

Tar-Míriel
(Ar-Zimraphel)
* 3117 ‡3319

Ar-Pharazôn
(Tar-Calion)
* 3118 ‡3319
●3255 ○3319

XIX Elendil
* 3119 ‡3441

s

Table 8: The Heirs of Elendil: Founding the Realms in Exile

2 Disaster of the Gladden Fields

This table displays the High Kings (as their claimed title is - less formally they are known as the Heirs of Isildur) of the Northern and the kings of the Southern Kingdom (also known as the Line of Anárion) until both suffered an important rupture of succession at about the same time.

The Northern Kingdom, Arnor, disintegrated by division among three sons: a habit resembling the collapse of Charlemagne's empire, with as fatal consequences for the subsequent history of each partial state. The first southern line faltered with Tarannon's clearly failed attempt to manifest the expansion of his realm by conquest *and* marriage: his wife, Beruthiel, was allegedly a Black Númenórean from the port of Umbar.

It seems an odd comment of fate that both sons of Elendil had four children and that in each case, the fourth child was the successor of his father. In Valandil's case, the reason is obvious because all three older brothers died on the Gladden Fields. It is not attested whether the same fate met Meneldil's older siblings nor whether they were boys or girls.

The famous longevity of the House of Elros was still to some extent preserved among the descendants of the Lords of Andunië. The average lifespan of their Northern line was as high as 230 years, that of the Southern line was even 260 years, while the length of a generation matches that found among the late Kings of Númenor: 91 years for the Northern line and 81 for the Southern.

This is hard to explain. As usual when Eru, the highest god, intervened, justice was elsewhere: Should he not have made a statement in his own favour by rewarding the Faithful with further granting them the original lifespan that the early descendants of Elros had enjoyed? Or why would *they,* who had no part in it, be punished for the Fall that the King's Men had committed?

The sons of Isildur are attested by **GF**; the sons of Anárion are found in **DG**. After Valandil and Meneldil, the genealogical tree follows **KR** that records only the ruling (male) descendants.

Death dates are given according to **KR**, birth dates according to **HE**.

420 Minas Anor rebuilt

490-500 Invasion of Easterlings

Stewardship of Gondor

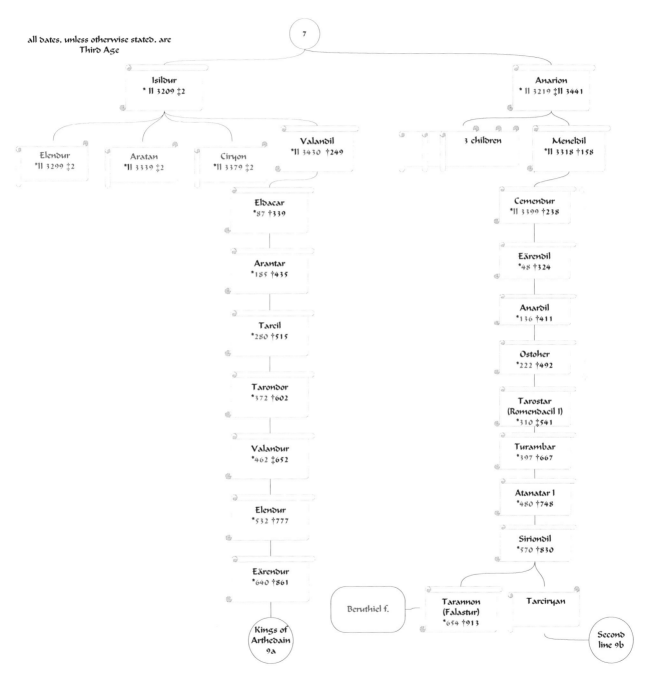

all dates, unless otherwise stated, are
Third Age

7

Isildur
* II 3209 ‡2

Anarion
* II 3219 ‡II 3441

Elendur
*II 3299 ‡2

Aratan
*II 3339 ‡2

Ciryon
*II 3379 ‡2

Valandil
*3430 †249

3 children

Meneldil
*II 3318 †158

Eldacar
*87 †339

Cemendur
*II 3399 †238

Arantar
*185 †435

Eärendil
*48 †324

Tarcil
*280 †515

Anardil
*136 †411

Tarondor
*372 †602

Ostoher
*222 †492

Valandur
*462 ‡652

Tarostar
(Romendacil I)
*310 ‡541

Elendur
*532 †777

Turambar
*397 †667

Eärendur
*640 †861

Atanatar I
*480 †748

Siriondil
*570 †830

Beruthiel f.

Tarannon
(Falastur)
*654 †913

Tarciryan

Kings of
Arthedain
9a

Second
line 9b

Table 9: The early kings of Arthedain and the second line of Gondor

After the division of Arnor into three successor kingdoms, only the kings of Arthedain have been recorded in the documents (**KR**), probably because they alone contributed to the ancestry of king Elessar of Gondor. The royal lines of Cardolan and Rhúdaur descended from the younger brothers of Amlaith of Fornost. Little more can be said about them beyond the general statement that both were recorded as perished in the year 1350 TA.

The Line of Isildur extinguished first in Rhúdaur. This former kingdom was then ruled by an undocumented hierarchy of lords of the 'evil Hillmen' that were vassals of the Witch-kingdom of Angmar and hostile to the other two Arnorian statelets. The Hillmen lords survived till 1975 TA.

The throne of Cardolan, it seems, was occupied by an unrecorded line of princes after the royal House had faded, probably by a marginal line of the Heirs of Isildur. Their last member fell in battle 1409 (**KR**) and was burrowed on the Harrow-Downs. It has been commonly assumed that his was the sword that killed the Witch-king on the Pelennor Fields.

The second line of the Heirs of Anárion ended when Narmacil I was succeeded by his own younger brother.

The lines of both kingdoms are marked by further decrease of the sequence of generations and gradual reduction of lifespans, especially in the North. The average expectancy of the kings of Arthedain shrank to 215 years, despite the alleged higher purity of their bloodline, while the Heirs of Anárion continued to enjoy about 250 years. It is noteworthy in this context that Dúnedainic kings have a tendency to fall in battle, if at all, when they are in high age, so that even their premature loss does not significantly speed up the sequence of succession. The change of generations was now about 85 years for Arthedain and reducing toward 70 years in Gondor.

Death dates are given according to **KR**, birth dates according to **HE**.

726 Division of Arnor

ca. 900 Pelargir rebuilt
933 Conquest of Umbar

ca. 1050 Harfoots in Eriador

ca. 1150 Fallohides

1050 Conquest of Harad

Waning of Gondor begins

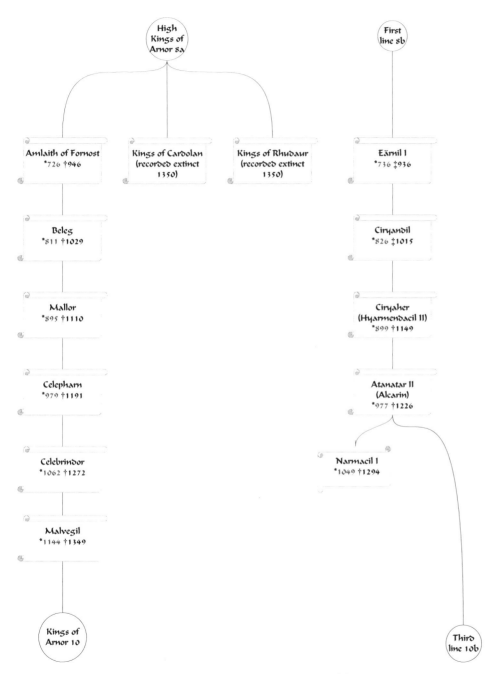

High Kings of Arnor 8a

First line 8b

Amlaith of Fornost
*726 †946

Kings of Cardolan
(recorded extinct 1350)

Kings of Rhudaur
(recorded extinct 1350)

Eärnil 1
*736 ‡936

Beleg
*811 †1029

Ciryandil
*826 ‡1015

Mallor
*895 †1110

Ciryaher
(Hyarmendacil II)
*899 †1149

Celepharn
*979 †1191

Atanatar II
(Alcarin)
*977 †1226

Celebrindor
*1062 †1272

Narmacil I
*1049 †1294

Malvegil
*1144 †1349

Kings of Arnor 10

Third line 10b

Table 10: Kings of Arnor restored, the third line of Gondor and the Lords of Umbar

When both the royal lines of Cardolan and Rhúdaur had failed, the current king of Arthedain, Argeleb I, boldly claimed kingship over the entire territory of former Arnor, though he wisely avoided to call himself High King. It is heeded little that also the state, Arthedain, reverted to applying the ancient name of Arnor to itself, including Cardolan, that submitted to the status of a satellite state run by 'princes', and Rhúdaur, that contested the claim. With the ultimate loss and desertion of Cardolan during the Great Plague of 1636, Argeleb II found new Arnor, again reduced to the boundaries of Arthedain, in a situation that could be compared to the realm of Syagrius in 5th century Gaul: a last remnant of ancient civilisation in a sea of foes.

When king Eldacar of the third southern line married beyond the confines of Gondor into the line of the king of Rhóvanion, Vidugavia [one might wonder how Eldacar felt when he lost his short-lived, non-Dúnedainic wife, watching her wither away very shortly after their marriage], the Kin-strife led to the secession of its southernmost province, Umbar, that established itself as a sovereign lordship. Its first ruler was the usurper and rebel Castamir who even held the throne of Gondor for a while. He was succeeded by a dynastic line of Dúnedainic lords (on the history of 'The Third Realm in Exile', Umbar and its lords, see the separate volume 'Middle-earth seen by the barbarians, Vol. 1'). Their last living descendants fell in battle against Umbardacil of Gondor.

The extraordinary longevity of the House of Elros still prevailed. While life expectancy stayed at 200 years in the North and almost 250 years in the South, the generations of the Gondorian lineage followed in more rapid succession, however. The average age of a king when his heir was born reduced to 60-65 years in Gondor. In new Arnor, one generation was still 80 years.

Death dates are given according to **KR**, birth dates according to **HE**.

1248 Defeat of Rhún
1250 Valacar as Ambassador in Rhóvanion

ca. 1300 Angmar established
ca. 1350 Arthedain claims Kingship of entire Arnor
1356 War of Arthedain and Rhúdaur

1409 Invasion by Angmar
Cardolan deserted

1432-1447 Kin-Strife

1540-1551 War against Harad/Umbar

1634 Pelargir ravaged

1636 Great Plague
1640 Osgiliath deserted

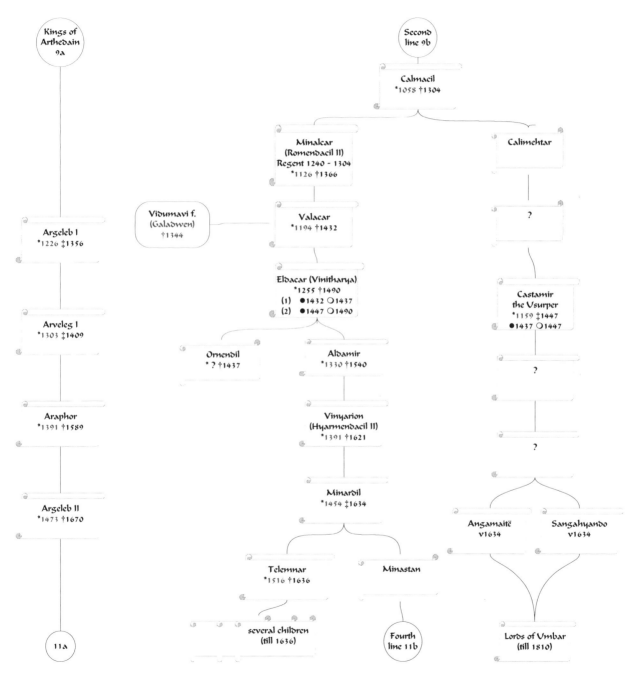

Kings of
Arthedain
9a

Second
line 9b

Calmacil
*1058 †1304

Minalcar
(Romendacil II)
Regent 1240 - 1304
*1126 †1366

Calimehtar

Vidumavi f.
(Galadwen)
†1344

Valacar
*1194 †1432

?

Argeleb 1
*1226 ‡1356

Eldacar (Vinitharya)
*1255 †1490
(1) ●1432 ○1437
(2) ●1447 ○1490

Castamir
the Usurper
*1159 ‡1447
●1437 ○1447

Arveleg 1
*1303 ‡1409

Ornendil
* ? †1437

Aldamir
*1330 †1540

?

Araphor
*1391 †1589

Vinyarion
(Hyarmendacil II)
*1391 †1621

?

Argeleb II
*1473 †1670

Minardil
*1454 ‡1634

Angamaitë
v1634

Sangahyando
v1634

Telemnar
*1516 †1636

Minastan

11a

several children
(till 1636)

Fourth
line 11b

Lords of Umbar
(till 1810)

Table 11: The Failure of the House of Elendil and the merger of its two Lines

Despite its political insignificance and its neglect by the much more powerful southern brethren of Gondor, shrunken new Arnor held out for another 300 years. The male line of Isildur continued without interruption till Arvedui, who bore the pessimistic epithet 'Last King' already in his name. Now both lines of the House of Elendil faded within a single (Dúnedainic) generation.

After the death of Ondoher and the extinction of all male members of the entire fourth line of Gondor, Arvedui was the first king of new Arnor to claim again High Kingship of all Dúnedain, referring not so much to his descent from Isildur, however, but to his marriage with Fíriel of Gondor who would by Númenórean law have been legitimate heiress of the fourth line. The claim was rejected with arguments based on Gondorian law. Arvedui survived the end of his kingship by a winter spent among the Lossoth. Whether Fíriel survived the war in which the North Kingdom perished is unknown.

Following the rejection of Arvedui's claim of High-Kingship, the senate of Gondor installed a short-lived fifth line that had only two members. When king Eärnur had vanished in Minas Morgul and was declared dead, rulership was granted to the House of Emyn Arnen that claimed descent from Elros but did not act as kings (see table 13).

The House of Elendil survived only in the North - most commonly referred to, as before, as the Line of Isildur. But actually, through Arvedui and Firiel, it constituted a merger and biological continuation of both the Lines of Isildur and Anárion that had run separately for almost exactly two milleniums.

Strangely, a further decrease of life expectancy set in right then, reducing the Northern Line to 175 years and the Southern Line to 200. In the South, the length of a generation shrank to about 52 years while it stayed virtually unchanged in the North.

Death dates are given according to **KR**, birth dates according to **HE**.

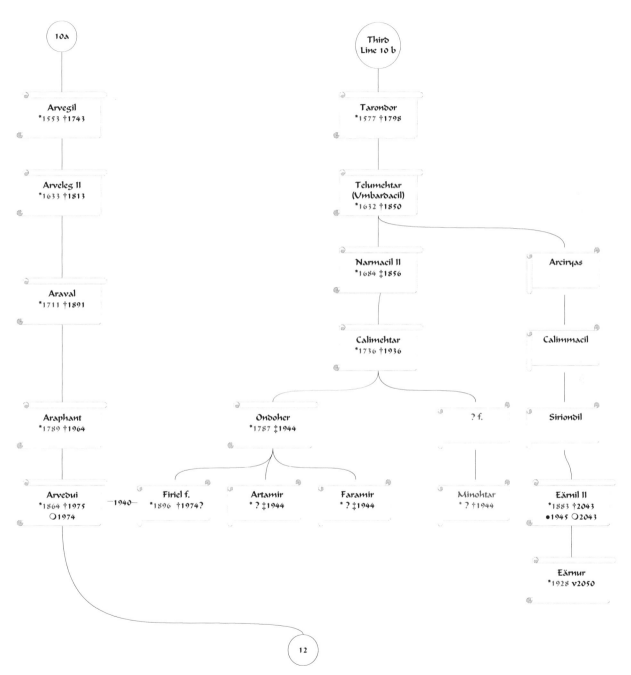

10a

Third
Line 10 b

Arvegil
*1553 †1743

Tarondor
*1577 †1798

Arveleg II
*1633 †1813

Telumehtar
(Umbardacil)
*1632 †1850

Araval
*1711 †1891

Narmacil II
*1684 ‡1856

Arciryas

Calimehtar
*1736 †1936

Calimmacil

Araphant
*1789 †1964

Ondoher
*1787 ‡1944

? f.

Siriondil

Arvedui
*1864 †1975
○1974

—1940—

Firiel f.
*1896 †1974?

Artamir
* ? ‡1944

Faramir
* ? ‡1944

Minohtar
* ? †1944

Eärnil II
*1883 †2043
●1945 ○2043

Eärnur
*1928 v2050

12

12: The Chieftains of the Rangers and the Kings of the Reunited Kingdom

The lines of Isildur and Anárion were at last reunited in Aranarth, first chieftain of the Dúnedain of the North who were now called *Rangers*. Recorders noted with surprise that the male descent continued uninterrupted for a full thousand years till Aragorn II (**KR**) who re-established the High Kingship of the Dúnedain, once forsaken by Amlaith of Fornost, as the first ruler of the Reunited Kingdom that comprised the territory of both Arnor and Gondor. (Though it is not obvious how much of Gondor was actually claimed beyond the territory it had under the last Ruling Stewards from the House of Emyn Arnen, see tables 13 et seq.: Ithilien, obviously, but also the long lost provinces of Umbar or Dorwinion?)

By marrying his aunt (much removed) Arwen Undómiel, grand-daughter of Eärendil, Aragorn also reunited the two lines of the Half-Elves that had separated with Elros and his brother Elrond. Beyond his son Eldarion and some daughters, unnamed, no members of the line of the Reunited Kingdom have been recorded any more.

Though a case could be made that the House of Isildur stayed most faithfully to Eru and the Valar while their lineage lasted, Eru yet continued to punish them for the Fall of Númenor - that their ancestors had fervently opposed - by reducing their life expectancy even further, down to 160 years or twice the span of other mortal men at their time. The one exception is Aragorn II who was extraordinarily long-lived, but it is not known whether he passed this trait on to his descendants. The period of a generation was still longer than Fíriel had known it, lingering around 70 years and then slowly dropping to 60 years till the end of the Third Age. Aragorn II, however, was way in his 100s when his heir Eldarion was born. The circumstances of his life and marriage had been very special, however.

Death dates are given according to **KR**, birth dates, unless recorded in **TY**, according to **HE**.

2460 End of Watchful Peace
2480 Orcs occupy Misty Mountains

2740-2747 Orcs invade Eriador
2758 Long Winter

2911 Fell Winter
2912 Tharbad ruined and deserted

3018-3019 War of the Ring
Return of the Kingdom
3022 Beginning of Fourth Age

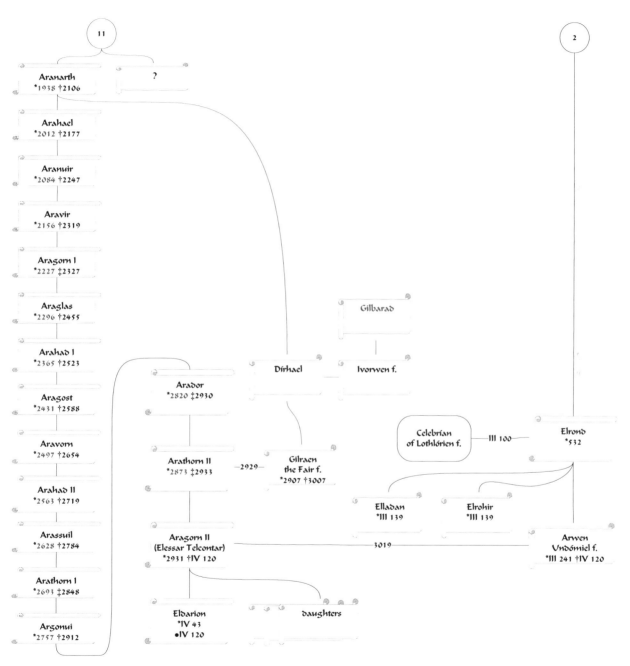

11

2

Aranarth
*1938 †2106

?

Arahael
*2012 †2177

Aranuir
*2084 †2247

Aravir
*2156 †2319

Aragorn I
*2227 ‡2327

Araglas
*2296 †2455

Gilbarad

Arahad I
*2365 †2523

Aragost
*2431 †2588

Arador
*2820 ‡2930

Dírhael

Ivorwen f.

Aravorn
*2497 †2654

Celebrían
of Lothlórien f.

III 100

Elrond
*532

Arahad II
*2563 †2719

Arathorn II
*2873 ‡2933

—2929—

Gilraen
the Fair f.
*2907 †3007

Arassuil
*2628 †2784

Elladan
*III 139

Elrohir
*III 139

Arathorn I
*2693 ‡2848

Aragorn II
(Elessar Telcontar)
*2931 †IV 120

—3019—

Arwen
Undómiel f.
*III 241 †IV 120

Argonui
*2757 †2912

Eldarion
*IV 43
•IV 120

daughters

Table 13: The first and second lines of the House of Emyn Arnen

HE is the only source which records that the male line of the House of Emyn Arnen was twice discontinued. It is also only here that we learn about Túrin's two marriages and various daughters who did not come into **KR,** for the sake of compression. No members of this dynasty are recorded prior to Húrin of Emyn Arnen. He is known to have been 'of royal descent' (**KR**), however, he was not a scion of the House of Elendil. In other words, his ancestors descended at some unknown time from the Line of Elros.

This assumption is supported by their average life expectancy and period of a generation. The Ruling Stewards are by no means as long-lived as the descendants of Elendil: On the average they live about 110-120 years and the change of generations is fast in comparison to the Lines of Isildur or Anárion: A typical Ruling Steward is about 40 years old when his heir is born. The period shrank to 30 years in the second line, approaching that of common mortal men. A notable

exception is Hador whose father was 80 in the year of his birth (though he was preceded by several daughters), and he enjoyed a life that lasted a full 150 years.

According to **HE,** the second line began with Denethor I, son of Rían daughter of Ruling Steward Barahir. Ecthelion I died childless and was succeeded by his nephew Egalmoth, founder of the third line.

Note that the Ruling Stewards have the habit to name their children for heroes of the First Age - though some of them, like Hallas, have not made it into the published **S,** their names have been retained as part of the legendarium.

The double marriage of Túrin I was recorded in his time already as 'rare and remarkable among the nobles of Gondor', and it is unheard of in the royal houses of the Edain or Dúnedain. Even Eldacar of Gondor who outlived his wife by several decades did not do that.

Death dates are given according to **KR**, birth dates according to **HE.**

ca. 1620 Steward chosen from Emyn Arnen

1980 Witch-king returns to Mordor
2000-2002 Minas Ithil besieged and conquered by Mordor

2050 End of the Line of Anárion Begin of the Rule of the Stewards

2063-2460 Watchful Peace

2475 Osgiliath finally ruined

2510 Balchoth wars; Oath of Eorl

2698 White Tower built in Minas Tirith

The Line of Elros

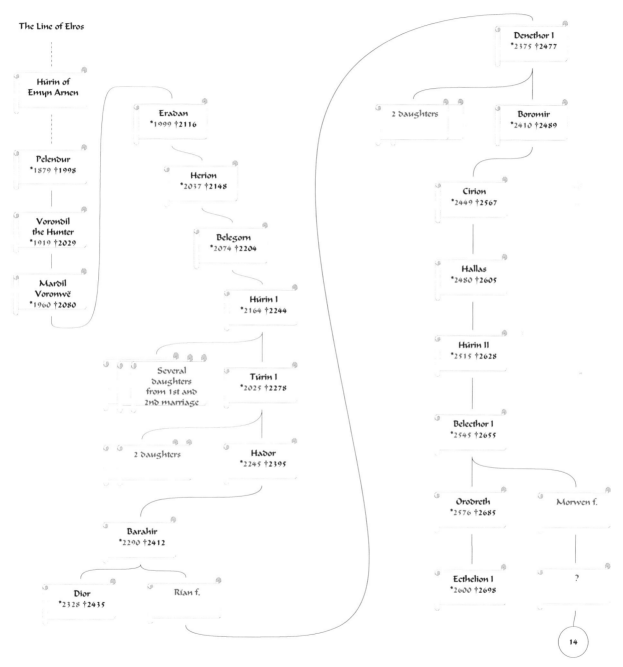

Húrin of
Emyn Arnen

Pelendur
*1879 †1998

Vorondil
the Hunter
*1919 †2029

Mardil
Voronwë
*1960 †2080

Eradan
*1999 †2116

Herion
*2037 †2148

Belegorn
*2074 †2204

Húrin I
*2164 †2244

Several
daughters
from 1st and
2nd marriage

Túrin I
*2025 †2278

2 daughters

Hador
*2245 †2395

Barahir
*2290 †2412

Dior
*2328 †2435

Rían f.

Denethor I
*2375 †2477

2 daughters

Boromir
*2410 †2489

Cirion
*2449 †2567

Hallas
*2480 †2605

Húrin II
*2515 †2628

Belecthor I
*2545 †2655

Orodreth
*2576 †2685

Morwen f.

Ecthelion I
*2600 †2698

?

14

Table 14: The third line of the House of Emyn Arnen and the Princes of Ithilien

There is no dramatic change to the life expectancy or the succession of generations among the Ruling Stewards of the third line, from Egalmoth to Denethor II.

When the Gondorian province of Ithilien was deserted in 2901 TA, the House of Húrin (as it was then more commonly called) lost its previous residence in Emyn Arnen. After more than a century, it was reconstituted by Faramir, who had briefly been last Ruling Steward and was granted the property of Emyn Arnen by king Aragorn II. The line he founded became known as the Princes of Ithilien.

It has sometimes been suspected that this gesture was unappreciative by king Aragorn, as if Faramir had deliberately been exiled, despite his taking part in constituting the king on his throne, to remove a potential competitor for political power. This is certainly not so, for the Princes of Ithilien retained the title of hereditary Stewards and Faramir stayed throughout his life a kind of chancellor to the realm: the most important political figure in Gondor after the king himself.

No further Prince of Ithilien was recorded after Faramir's grandson Barahir who is mainly known as author of the 'Tale of Aragorn and Arwen'.

Death dates are given according to **KR**, birth dates, where not recorded in **TY**, according to **HE**.

Problems and discrepancies

Belecthor II: His date of death is recorded in **KR** and **HE** as 2872, but in **TY** it was erroneously stated as 2852. This has been amended in editions after 2005.

Finduilas: Died 2987 in **HE** but in 2988 according to TY.

Barahir: He is not explicitly stated anywhere as a son of Elboron, son of Faramir. But no other children of Faramir are known, hence, this interpretation is likely.

2758 Long Winter; Corsair attack

2852 White Tree dies

2885 Battle of Poros
2901 Ithilien deserted. Henneth Annûn founded

2951 Sauron declares himself

2954 Mount Doom erupts

3018-3019 War of the Ring
End of the Stewardship
3022 Fourth Age begins

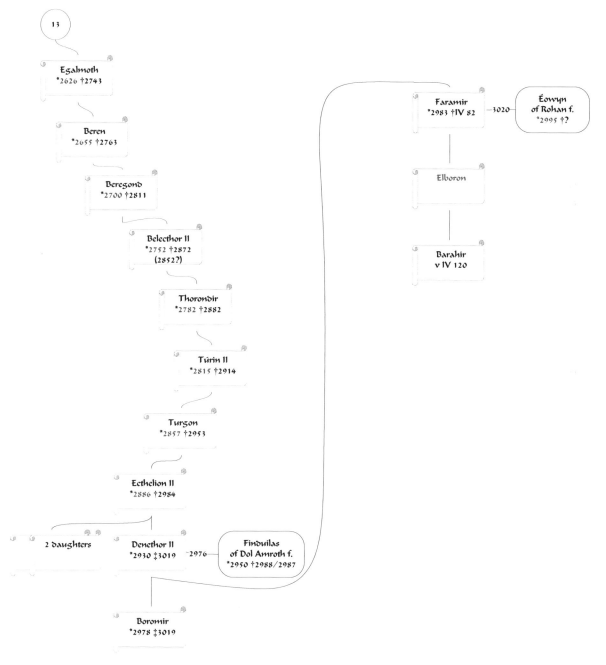

13

Egalmoth
*2626 †2743

Beren
*2655 †2763

Beregond
*2700 †2811

Belecthor II
*2752 †2872
(2852?)

Thorondir
*2782 †2882

Túrin II
*2815 †2914

Turgon
*2857 †2953

Ecthelion II
*2886 †2984

2 daughters

Denethor II
*2930 ‡3019

—2976—

Finduilas
of Dol Amroth f.
*2950 †2988/2987

Boromir
*2978 ‡3019

Faramir
*2983 †IV 82

—3020—

Éowyn
of Rohan f.
*2995 †?

Elboron

Barahir
v IV 120

Table 15: The Princes of Dol Amroth

The actual origin of the house of Dol Amroth is contested. The oldest ancestor recorded is a man named Adrahil of Dol Amroth who participated in the Battle of the Camp, 1944 TA (**CE**). If that was true, he may have been the father of Imrazôr the Númenórean. (Note that this Imrazôr bore an Adûnaic name despite the low esteem of this language in Gondor, as do his remote descendants Adrahil and Imrahil.)

Alas, Imrazôr is elsewhere stated to be the founder of Dol Amroth - and inventor of its name (**CE, HE**)! According to these sources, his wife was the Elf Mithrellas whose physical features were still visible in her remote descendant Imrahil, recognised by Legolas, especially by the lack of any beard-growth which is allegedly 'a characteristic of all Elves' (despite the considerable beard that Círdan the Shipwright sported). One may wonder what should have distinguished the descendants of Mithrellas the Elf from those of Elwing the Elf: should not all the lineage of Elros have been beardless as well, including Aragorn and Boromir? Or was Elros' decision to become a man rewarded with a lifelong and unprecedented - for someone with Elvish roots - need to shave? (Along comes Elrond the morning after: 'You ought to have a look in that mirror, dear brother. And better get yourself a sharp knife before you come downstairs for breakfast.')

The records of the Princes of Dol Amroth (**HE)** provide a curious phenomenon: in most cases, the dates are known but not the names. For convenience, they have been numbered in sequential order here, as has been the case with the unnamed Lords of Anduníe. It may be noted that it was Prince IX who witnessed the Oath of Eorl (**CE**).

Morwen Steelsheen was born and raised in Lossarnach but descended from one of the Princes of Dol Amroth (**KR**). His identity or sequential number in the dynasty has not been attested.

Problems and discrepancies

Finduilas: A slightly deviant date of her death is given in **HE**.

1980 Witch-king returns to Mordor

2000-2002 Minas Ithil besieged and conquered by Mordor

2050 End of the Line of Anárion

2475 Osgiliath finally ruined

2510 Balchoth wars;
Oath of Éorl

2698 White Tower built in Minas Tirith
2758 Long Winter; Corsair attack
2852 White Tree dies

2885 Battle of Poros

2901 Ithilien deserted. Henneth Annûn founded

2951 Sauron declares himself
2954 Mount Doom erupts

3018-3019 War of the Ring
3022 Beginning of the Fourth Age

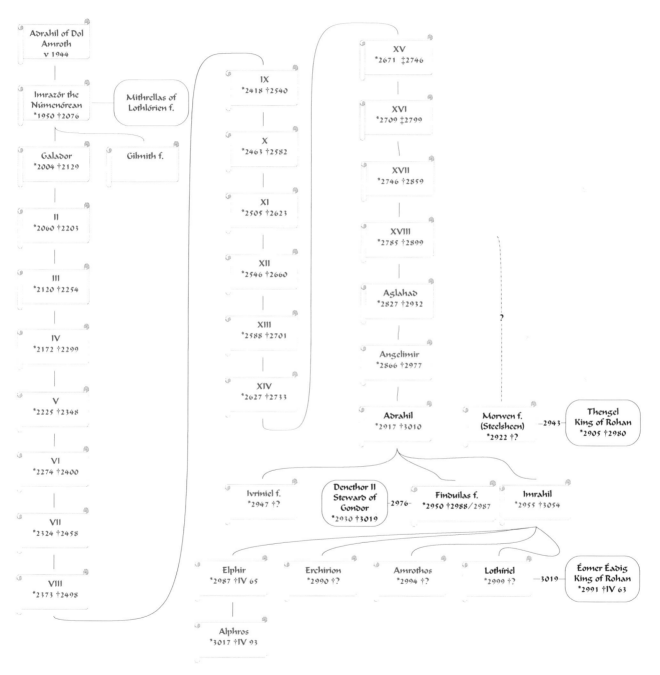

Adrahil of Dol Amroth
v 1944

Imrazôr the Númenórean
*1950 †2076

Mithrellas of Lothlórien f.

Galador
*2004 †2129

Gilmith f.

II
*2060 †2203

III
*2120 †2254

IV
*2172 †2299

V
*2225 †2348

VI
*2274 †2400

VII
*2324 †2458

VIII
*2373 †2498

IX
*2418 †2540

X
*2463 †2582

XI
*2505 †2623

XII
*2546 †2660

XIII
*2588 †2701

XIV
*2627 †2733

XV
*2671 ‡2746

XVI
*2709 ‡2799

XVII
*2746 †2859

XVIII
*2785 †2899

Aglahad
*2827 †2932

Angelimir
*2866 †2977

Adrahil
*2917 †3010

?

Morwen f. (Steelsheen)
*2922 †?

—2943—

Thengel King of Rohan
*2905 †2980

Ivriniel f.
*2947 †?

Denethor II Steward of Gondor
*2930 †3019

—2976—

Finduilas f.
*2950 †2988/2987

Imrahil
*2955 †3054

Elphir
*2987 †IV 65

Erchirion
*2990 †?

Amrothos
*2994 †?

Lothíriel
*2999 †?

—3019—

Éomer Éadig King of Rohan
*2991 †IV 63

Alphros
*3017 †IV 93

Table 16: Lords of the Éothéod, the first line of Rohan and the origin of the Lords of Aldburg

The Lords of the Éothéod claimed descent from Vidugavia, self-styled 'King of Rhovanion' in the time of king Eldacar. They were, however, removed from him by many generations and the claim remains unverified. According to **CE** at least, Lord Marhari is explicitly named 'a descendant of Vidugavia'. This King of Rhovanion must have been a very prominent character in the history of Wilderland indeed, though little is known about him: Gondor even sent its throne heir as ambassador to his (unidentified) residence. Yet his claim to rule all Rhovanion may have been exaggerating.

The line of the Lords of the Éothéod is only known in excerpts. The descendants of Marhwini (**CE**) ruled not only the Éothéod proper but an entire confederation of tribes in Rhóvanion. There were probably two or more generations between his line and their descendant Frumgar, who led his people to the upper vales of Anduin in 1977. His son Fram founded Framsburg, that remained capital of the Éothéod till the emigration of 2510.

Ruling Steward Cirion of Emyn Arnen granted Gondor's northwestern province, Calenardhon, to Eorl who established himself there not only as Lord of the Mark but as a sovereign king - probably modelled not so much on the role of Vidugavia but on the by then extinct royal line of Gondor. Was assuming this title a deliberate pun against the Ruling Stewards who were not entitled to kingship?

The first line ended when Helm Hammerhand and his heirs were killed in the Long Winter, during the fight against the usurper Wulf whose father claimed descent from king Fréawine of Rohan. In Helm's case, the word 'line' is to be taken literally, for the line of mounds that covered the deceased kings of Rohan was ended with Helm and a second line started.

The origin of the Lords of Aldburg is attested only in **CE**. All dates are given according to **KR**.

1248 Gondor defeats Rhún

1250 Valacar as Ambassador in Rhóvanion
1432-1447 Kin-Strife
1636 Great Plague

1851 Wainrider invasion begins
1899 Battle of Dagorlad

before 1936: Éothéod first time recorded

1944 Battle of the Camp.

1977 Frumgar leads Éothéod north

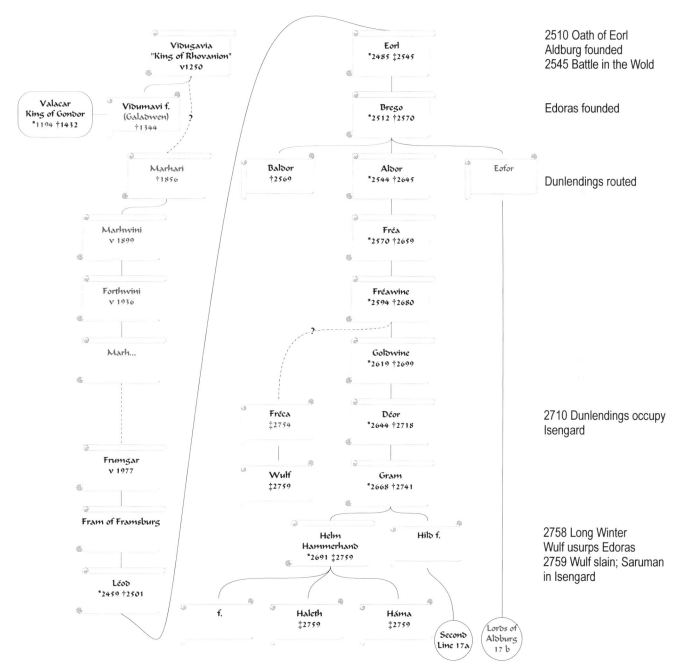

Vidugavia "King of Rhovanion" v1250

Valacar King of Gondor *1194 †1432

Vidumavi f. (Galadwen) †1344

Marhari †1856

Marhwini v 1899

Forthwini v 1936

Marh...

Frumgar v 1977

Fram of Framsburg

Léod *2459 †2501

Eorl *2485 ‡2545

Brego *2512 †2570

Baldor †2569

Aldor *2544 †2645

Eofor

Fréa *2570 †2659

Fréawine *2594 †2680

Goldwine *2619 †2699

Fréca ‡2754

Déor *2644 †2718

Wulf ‡2759

Gram *2668 †2741

Helm Hammerhand *2691 ‡2759

Hild f.

f.

Haleth ‡2759

Háma ‡2759

Second Line 17a

Lords of Aldburg 17 b

2510 Oath of Eorl
Aldburg founded
2545 Battle in the Wold

Edoras founded

Dunlendings routed

2710 Dunlendings occupy Isengard

2758 Long Winter
Wulf usurps Edoras
2759 Wulf slain; Saruman in Isengard

Table 17: The second and third lines of Rohan and the Lords of Aldburg

2806-64 Orcs raid in Rohan

The second line of the kings of Rohan ended with Théoden whose son and heir, Théodred, fell even before him in the War of the Ring.

The third line was established by the Lord of Aldburg, who was never named as such in any record but evidently bore the title since the death of his father, Éomund, who was otherwise known as deriving from Eastfold. Éomer Lord of Aldburg happened to be the king's nephew through his mother. He was hence second to Théodred in the line of succession.

No successors of Éomer's son Elfwine, cousin of Elboron, Prince of Emyn Arnen, have been recorded. Note that here, the name reappears that, spelt Aelfwine, has long prevailed in the tradition as belonging to that man who recorded the Book of Lost Tales, or the Quenta Silmarillion, or the Silmarillion proper, during a visit to the island of Tol Eressëa. This would have been an impossible feat for Elfwine King of Rohan and official tradition has it that the Silmarillion was popularised by Bilbo Baggins instead who translated a copy in Rivendell. Still, it seems remarkable that Éomer would name his son 'Elf-friend', though even in the War of the Ring he did not develop a particularly close relationship to Elves whom he merely respected for their fighting skills. The choice of name may yet be more significant than meets the eye.

Note that Elfwine had the epithet 'the Fair'. Perhaps he was more similar to his mother, Lothíriel of Dol Amroth, who originated from a house that was already related to the kings of Rohan through his great-grandmother, Morwen Steelsheen.

All dates except for Lothíriel's birth-date (that is found in **HE**) are given according to **KR**.

2885 Battle of Poros

Problems and discrepancies

Walda: his death date is recorded in **KR** as 2851 but it was given as 2861 in **TY**. This discrepancy has been amended neither in the revision of 2004 nor in that of 2005.

3014 Gríma gains Théoden's favour
3018-3019 War of the Ring

3019 Oath of Éorl confirmed by Éomer Éadig

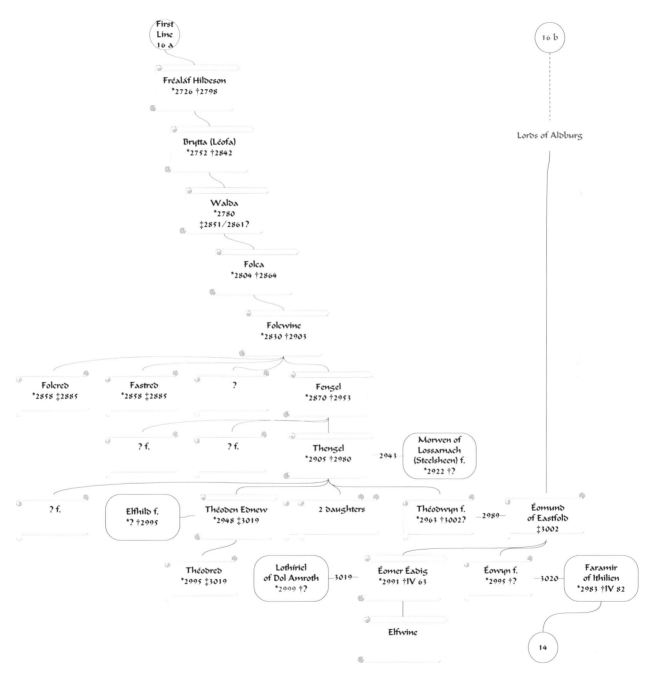

First
Line
16 a

16 b

Fréaláf Hildeson
*2726 †2798

Lords of Aldburg

Brytta (Léofa)
*2752 †2842

Walda
*2780
‡2851/2861?

Folca
*2804 †2864

Folcwine
*2830 †2903

Folcred
*2858 ‡2885

Fastred
*2858 ‡2885

?

Fengel
*2870 †2953

? f.

? f.

Thengel
*2905 †2980

2943

Morwen of
Lossarnach
(Steelsheen) f.
*2922 †?

? f.

Elfhild f.
*? †2995

Théoden Ednew
*2948 ‡3019

2 daughters

Théodwyn f.
*2963 †3002?

2989

Éomund
of Eastfold
‡3002

Théodred
*2995 ‡3019

Lothíriel
of Dol Amroth
*2999 †?

3019

Éomer Éadig
*2991 †IV 63

Éowyn f.
*2995 †?

3020

Faramir
of Ithilien
*2983 †IV 82

Elfwine

14

Table 15: The last Lords and first Kings of Dale

The earliest record of the existence of Men of Dale dates from 1944 TA (**CE**). The town so named, however, was apparently founded when Thrór II was king of the Dwarves in the halls beneath Erebor from 2590 to 2770 TA (**H, KR**). It has often been argued that the Lords of Dale were actually kings and even, sometimes, that they descended from Vidugavia, that self-styled King of Rhovanion long, long ago. But neither claim is supported by any statement in the extant texts: the lords of Dale are lords and only that and the matter of having a king seems to have been a spontaneous demand of *vox populi* that did not relate to previous tradition - up to that point, the golden age of the dwarvish King under the Mountains had been kept in memory but not that of any mannish king of Dale.

Only the last Lord of Dale, Girion, is recorded by name, and how many Lords preceded him is unknown. His wife and children (at least one of them had been adult at that point) outlived his death in the assault of Smaug the Golden. It is remarkable that Girion's name is a sample of early Elvish, probably derived from a Gnomish *gîrin*, 'bygone, old, belonging to ancient days, etc.' that has not survived into Sindarin. It may seem that this was not Girion's actual name but an epithet whose significance escaped Bilbo Baggins' notice.

Bard I., his direct descendant, was first proclaimed King of Dale and founder of the dynasty that succeeded him. Of this line, **TY** records only the death dates, alas.

One king too much

None of the tables displayed in this book is capable of integrating the illustrious king Bladorthin who is mentioned in **H** and only there. Despite his Elvish-looking name, he was almost certainly not an Elf but very likely a late descendant of the Line of Elros, though his name is not interpretable in the Elvish languages that had been spoken by the Dúnedain. For where his realm was likely located and what significance Bladorthin had in the history of the present tables, see the volume 'Middle-earth seen by the barbarians, Vol. 1'.

2590 Erebor founded
Dale built
Reign of King Bladorthin

2770 Smaug destroys Dale
End of Lordship of Dale

2941 Death of Smaug
Kingdom of Dale founded
2944 Rebulding of Dale begun

Kingdom of Dale expands along Celduin/Carnen

Dale expands South and East
3018-3019 War of the Ring

Lords of Dale

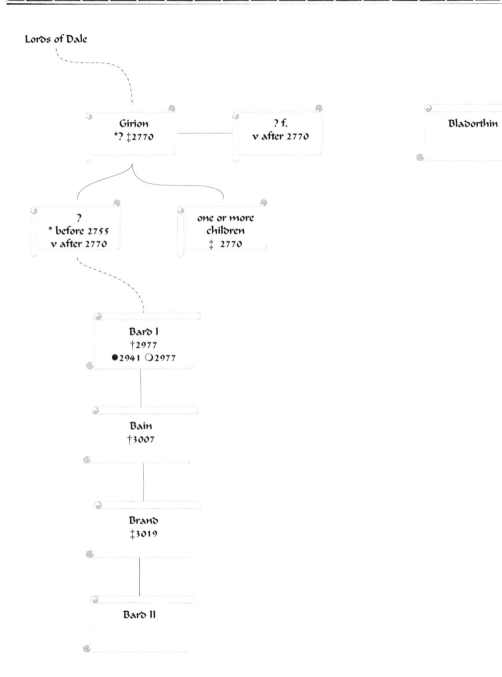

Girion
*? ‡2770

? f.
v after 2770

Bladorthin

?
* before 2755
v after 2770

one or more
children
‡ 2770

Bard I
†2977
●2941 ○2977

Bain
†3007

Brand
‡3019

Bard II

Other selected essays from
Lalaith's Middle-earth Science Pages

Middle-earth seen by the barbarians

How the Mannish peoples who lost the wars may have perceived the history of Middle-earth.

Vol 1: The indigenous peoples of Eriador and Condor
Vol 2: The lost history of the Men of Darkness in Rhún and Harad

Words of Westernesse

The development of grammar and vocabulary of the Mannish languages of Middle-earth and some tentative etymologies of Adûnaic and Westron

The Moon in 'The Hobbit'

How Tolkien used the moon as a narrative agent and how you can do that in your novel, too

All books include many illustrations, maps and diagrams.
Available in English as ebooks or printed.

When the last surviving sibling of the Antikythera Mechanism is stolen, the Roman Empire tumbles into a crisis of unprecedented scope. In the wrong hands, this most powerful instrument of the ancient world could have the political impact of a nuclear bomb under control of barbarian terrorists.

And so, in the seemingly peaceful period between the defeat of the Jewish rebel Bar-Kochba and the Parthian War, the rotten core of the Empire is exposed as powers long dismissed struggle for Imperial purple. A sectist astrologer establishes himself in the Germanic north and surrounds himself with murderers and terrorists. The fallen kingdom of Commagene is raising its dangerous head again. And beyond the border to the barbary lands, a criminal mastermind is craving for the stolen object - and for the man who knows how to use it.

The House of Iulii, a family from the border toward Germania, is forced to assume a key role in defending the emperors of Rome.

The ROMANIKE Series

Six volumes - one story!

Order from:
www.codex-regius.de

More essays on **Lalaith's Middle-earth Science Pages**:
http://homepage.o2mail.de/lalaith/M-earth.html

Order from:

www.corpus-sacrum.de

www.opus-gemini.de

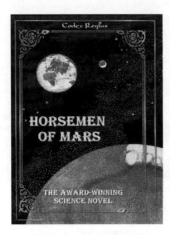

The Horsemen of Mars come with the solar wind.

The sparks beneath their invisible hoofs
illuminate the nights of the red planet.
A marvellous sight from the safety of
your base on Mars.

But when you are lost in the red planet's desert,
the Horsemen of Mars show their fatal facet
as their wild hunt is tracking down
your fragile body.

Join our Mars crew in the most critical
time of their mission! Follow them into
the struggle for their lives on the hostile
plains and hills of the red planet.

An illustrated science novel for
young and adult armchair astronomers.
Including two double-page maps and
many full-colour images from Mars' surface.

Award-winning in Germany – now also in English!

See the book trailer on Dailymotion or YouTube!

They called him Raven because he unravelled mankind's future - the future of a human species that had forgotten its past.
Only fragments of history in space have been preserved.
And the planet called Earth had been forgotten.

From Robots to Foundations

The most detailed timeline of all books and short-stories that Isaac Asimov set in the Robots-Foundation-Universe.

166 pages. 44 images and star maps.
ISBN-10: 1499569823
ISBN-13: 978-1499569827

See the video trailer on Dailymotion or YouTube!

No, the question where Atlantis
may have been is not answered.

Instead, the four friends discussing in this book wonder
where the author of the tale of Atlantis may have got his
inspirations from. Which function have the elements of his
narrative for the plot? Why are the kings who founded Atlantis five pairs of twins? Is a network of canals that would
have covered half of Germany technically feasible? And what
insights did Plato gain from erosion and environmental de-
struction that he was able to observe?

Atlantica: What Plato did not say

Forthcoming in winter 2015.
440 pages.
40 images.

See our publishing programme at:
www.codex-regius.de

In the sands of the Moon, at a place called the Marsh of
Decay, there lies an item which should not have been there.
It is a tiny figurine, shaped to look like a man, and he is dead.
Behind him, a plaque is set in the soil, bearing fourteen
names. Some are American, some Russian. This figurine was
called the Fallen Astronaut. The crew of Apollo 15 took it
there, without knowledge of their superiors, and they placed
it at this site to commemorate their colleagues from two
countries whom doom had struck before men landed on the
Moon. But there are more names than these, others which
are not even mentioned on that plaque, and knowledge
of their unhappy fates was lost. These men are

the Forgotten Astronauts ,

who were chosen to write history. But history passed over
them, sometimes tragically, sometimes tragicomically. Their
stories tell a darker chapter of the American moon-landings.
It is recounted in this book. With many full-colour images.

Order from:
www.codex-regius.de

Codex Regius is a pen name and label of a pair of two authors from Slovenia and Germany, respectively. One is a university engineer of chemistry and has spent her time trying to convey the wonders of the Periodic Table to mostly unreceptive students. The other, a graduate of physical engineering, has been working as a technical editor before both of them set up a freelance translation business together. Today they are working from home, which the children find very convenient when they come from school. The two authors of **Codex Regius** are married to each other and still trying to find a common language.

Please, visit our blog on **www.codex-regius.de** where we are regularly publishing news and background informations on our publishing programme.

Made in the USA
Monee, IL
06 December 2021

84104674R00030